CHAPTERS

1.	THE BIG-HAIRED MAN	4
2.	INVISIBLE ST-INK	14
3.	THE TOILET ROLL EXCHANGE	22
4.	JAWS!	30
5.	KNIGHT! KNIGHT!	40
6.	THE WHIFFY HOSTAGE	50
7.	THE (ENTIRELY LEGAL) CAR CHASE	60
8.	JAWS EXPLAINS IT ALL	72

THE SPY ZONE   82

This is no ordinary book! Each chapter's title-page contains either a 'Mission-ogram' or a 'Code-ogram' with a mission to be completed or code to be solved. Good luck and keep your wits about you.

CODE-OGRAM

YOU MUST CRACK THIS CODE
AND FIND THE HIDDEN
MESSAGE. STOP.

!TUOTIGNIKROWROFENODLLEW

END.

(Solution: Re-write the message starting with the last letter and working back to the first.)

4

CHAPTER 1

THE BIG-HAIRED MAN

Young Ralph was not that popular –
this everybody knew,
Especially 'The Coolest Kids',
who thought him someone who . . .
Was really quite 'unusual', though chivalrous and kind.
And, truth be told, Ralph knew all this, but really didn't mind.

Besides, our Ralph was brushing up his chess skills –
night and day.
His entry was accepted and he soon was going to play
In the 'Under-Fifteen European Chess Champs' – that weekend!
(But, being eight, would have to take 'a relative or friend'.)

'You want me to go WHERE?' his sister answered, in disgust.
'I'd rather stay at home and help Mum IRON, COOK or DUST!'
"But I must bring a relative because I'm under ten . . .
And you know you've always fancied dating European men."

'That's true,' his sister told him. 'Foreign accents do appeal.'
"And I'll buy lunch," Ralph added, as he tried to clinch the deal.

"Perhaps you might find one or two are worthy of a date . . .
Then I can introduce you, sis – just think of me as bait!"

But little did Ralph know, as he sat reading books that day,
That in a secret bunker, many hundred miles away,
A dark and bony figure, fuelled by jealousy and hate,
Was heading up a meeting to discuss our hero's fate!

'There's something wrong! There HAS to be!'
he told the other men.
'For nobody could play that well, yet still be under ten!
His moves aren't just ingenious – he plans out every stage
With all the skill and knowledge of a man six times his age!'

'So tell us, boss, what should we do?' a nervous voice replied.
'THE TIME HAS COME, AT LAST, MY FRIENDS!'
the darkened figure cried.
'The championships are next weekend,
we have to seize our chance . . .
To see this BOY in action!' he spat out, in angry stance.

'We need to send an agent, and he has to be our best
And here I've written down ONE name that stands
out from the rest.
For at The Chess Academy, such cheating's not condoned[1],
But if Ralph REALLY is this good – we must know HOW!'
he groaned.

---

[1] See Spy Zone page 92.

And so that next weekend our hero headed (sis in tow)
For the venue's *'Players' Entrance'* where the invite said to go.
Ralph quickly checked his number and then entered
the great hall,
Where one would end the victor –
but the rest were sure to fall.

He stared around the room at all the champions that he'd seen
On the 'Very Hard to Beat' page of his *Chess Champs* magazine,
But Lady Luck was nowhere near, as sitting at Ralph's board
Was the undisputed champion . . . Monsieur Grandfromage
. . . (Jean-Claude).

His English was impressive, with an accent thick and strong.
His clothes were neat and stylish and his hair was slick
and long.
'He's gorgeous!' said one woman, edging closer, just a fraction.
(Ralph soon surmised[2] his cunning play was not the main
attraction!)

---

[2] See Spy Zone page 93.

The two shook hands so forcefully,
Ralph quickly checked for bruising.
'I'm last year's champ . . .' Jean-Claude began
'. . . and I'm not big on losing!'
Ralph gulped a little as he checked his pawns were all in place,
Then banged his clock – the game began – at quite a speedy pace!

Ralph held his nerve, but mid-game
Jean-Claude made a huge mistake . . .
And lost his Queen to Ralph, who did a silent double-take.
"Perhaps it's all that aftershave! It must have thrown his game!"
Then Jean-Claude knocked his King down,
passing Ralph the victory flame!

'You must be French, my friend?' Jean-Claude began,
with knowing smile.
'Suspicions were aroused as I observed your playing style.
Your moves are so ingenious, perhaps you trained in France
Under the expert guidance of my master, Monsieur Clance?'

'They're saying that you WON, Ralph?'
said his sister, quite confused.
'*Oui, Mademoiselle* . . . it's true –
your *boyfriend* leaves my ego bruised!

I am Jean-Claude – now
tell me, please, just how
could it be true
That anyone not-French
could be as *très jolie*
as you?'

'My BROTHER,
not my BOYFRIEND!' said his sister. 'Yes, I'm single.
I came to watch Ralph play, but now he's won, I'm free to mingle.'
'Perhaps a cup of coffee?' said Jean-Claude. 'Or maybe dinner?
I'd love to spend some time with you –
and Ralph, our worthy winner!'

But back at the Headquarters of The Chess Academy,
A darkened figure watched it all on 'Spy CCTV'.
'It's all progressing nicely – Ralph, you've clearly not a clue . . .
What all my cunning colleagues here have got in store for
YOU!'

13

POST ✪ OFFICE
TELEGRAM

MISSION-OGRAM

YOU MUST INVENT THE
ULTIMATE SPY GADGET. STOP.

THINK OF A NAME FOR YOUR
GADGET. STOP.

HOW WILL IT LOOK AND HOW
IT WILL WORK? END.

CHAPTER 2

INVISIBLE ST-INK

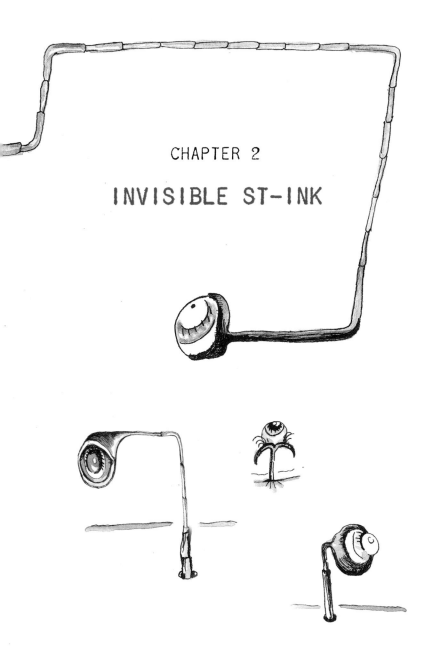

Ralph slept that night,
    still clutching his new trophy by his side.
    Though fast asleep, his face still shone with
happiness and pride.
His dreams were full of flashbacks to the previous day of glory,
Though sadly to Jean-Claude as well (the downside of the story!).

Ralph glided down to breakfast, with his trophy still in tow
In case a neighbour popped around and he'd be forced to show
It. 'Here he is . . .' Ralph's mum began '. . . my clever little son.'
'Get over it!' Ralph's sister snarled. 'We got it, right?
YOU WON!'

"Now, jealousy's an ugly trait, dear sister," he began.
"You're just upset I beat that suave[1] but highly scented man!
It may console you when I let you know that – all night long –
My dreams were plagued by Jean-Claude's cry:
'Ralph's French – I'm never wrong!'"

'*Bonjour, mes amis*,' Jean-Claude said, while pulling up a chair.
'There's coffee here,' Ralph's mum replied.
'And, please . . . do call me Claire.'
Ralph's sister smirked, as poor Ralph's eyebrows
hovered overhead.
'That's right, I've come to stay, Ralph, on your comfy sofa bed!'

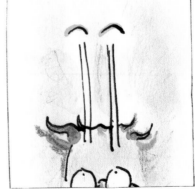

---

[1] See Spy Zone page 93.

'He's not my type of fella.' Ralph's dad whispered, out of range,
'Your mum and sis just LOVE this French attention for
a change!
But still, he'll help their language skills which, Ralph,
you must agree,
Will benefit us on our next French holiday . . . you'll see.'

And Jean-Claude said, 'I've cleared it with my school
and parents too,
They're all so glad I've found a lovely family like you!
And in a day or two, we'll be so cosy, never fear . . .
I'll blend in so completely that you'll soon forget I'm here!'

"I find that most unlikely," muttered Ralph,

and turned to leave.

"There must be more to this – there's something up his sleeve!"

And saw a message scribbled underneath his bowl, in pen:

'MEET ME – WILL EXPLAIN IT ALL – YOUR DINING

ROOM – IN TEN.'

Nine minutes, fifty seconds later, Ralph approached the door.

Inside, Jean-Claude marched up and down upon the wooden floor.

'Do come in, Ralph, take a seat – I'm glad you came ALONE,

But still I'll need to search you – and to check your

mobile phone . . .

For what I am to tell you is for just your ears, my friend.'
"Keep talking," answered Ralph. "The truth will come out
in the end . . .
I don't know if we're starring in some strange television show –
But writing on Mum's crockery is NOT the way to go!"

'RELAX! Just seconds later, Ralph, the message disappears.
It's special ink . . . it's safe . . . and I've been using it for years!
With someone so intelligent, I really should have known . . .
You'd quickly grow suspicious and my cover would be blown!

The truth is this, no matter what you've read in all your books,
There's so much more to me than flowing locks and
dashing looks.
You find me strange and too familiar – this, my friend, is why –
I'm sent here undercover, Ralph, I'm actually . . . A SPY!

We know The Chess Academy are jealous of your skill –
We've lots of proof and evidence they wish you only ill.
There's further information that I feel I must impart . . .
They plan to "take you out", Ralph, with a tranquillising[2] dart!

---

[2] See Spy Zone page 93.

It's not just YOU they're after, Ralph, but your big sister too.
To fathom your chess secrets, they might kidnap HER – it's true!
I'm sent here to protect you both and see you meet no harm.
I hope this information hasn't caused you great alarm?'

"But my sis doesn't know ONE THING about the game of chess!"
'That's obvious, my friend, but they would take her nonetheless.
And if you don't co-operate and give them what they need,
They'll hold your sis to ransom – it's their favourite evil deed!

'So from now on, TRUST NOBODY, they might be friend or foe.
I'm not just talking strangers, even people that you know!
I'll be here to protect you and to teach you how to be . . .
Alert to every threat, a wise and cunning spy – like me!'

MISSION-OGRAM

YOU MUST CRACK THIS CODE
AND FIND THE HIDDEN
MESSAGE. STOP.

TRMAFLJPOH'BS
CSTUFRZNWALMPE FIRS
DLHEPMXOGN

END.

22

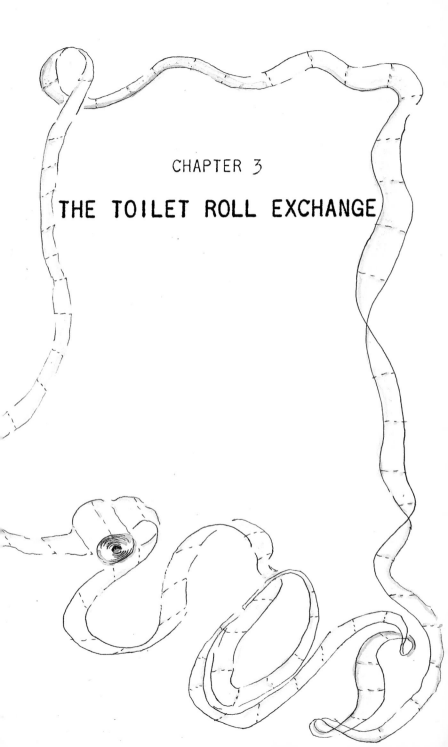

CHAPTER 3

THE TOILET ROLL EXCHANGE

Next day, Ralph and their visitor set off
for school at eight.
(Ralph planned to take the tourist route
and hated being late.)
He showed Jean-Claude the park and then their
local village shop,
Where Ruth (the narcoleptic[1]) slept beside her lollipop.

In front of all the school the Head said welcome to their guest,
Then spoke to him in French, which left the pupils quite
impressed!
Ralph heard the girls all whisper, 'Jean-Claude's GORGEOUS!'
. . . 'Is he taken?'
(All rivals to his sister's plan, if Ralph was not mistaken.)

They went on to the classroom, though this journey took a while.
Each time they passed a window, Jean-Claude stopped to
check his smile.
Then Ralph saw something curious, and wondered . . .
was he sane?
'BEWARE THE BIG CHEESE' written on the final window pane.

---

[1] See Spy Zone page 93.

"Big Cheese? . . . Er, that means Grandfromage?"

Ralph glanced towards Jean-Claude . . .

Who was entering the classroom and already looking bored.

"There's something going on here and I'm forced to question why

He doesn't try to blend more if he's actually a spy?"

Ralph glanced back to the message, muttering,

"This is getting WEIRD,"

As only seconds later all the words had disappeared!

"What strange occurrence will be next? . . . I haven't got a clue!"

(He wished his girlfriend, Amy, wasn't absent with the 'flu.)

Before long lunchtime came around and Jean-Claude

was surrounded,

Ralph thought it must grow tiresome – this always being hounded.

He peered across at Jean-Claude,
over *Chess Champs* magazine,
And wondered if the girls would flock
to RALPH by age fourteen?

Ralph scooped up both his plate and dish and put them
on his tray
(The school rules state: *'You must return your dishes every day'*),
But did a silent double-take as, written on his plate,
Was: 'Meet me in the loos in five – and, Ralph, do NOT be late!'

"Will people PLEASE stop writing on my crockery?" he said.
"There must be other ways to pass me messages instead!"
He watched the writing disappear and glanced around the hall,
But nobody looked guilty or suspicious there at all!

So Ralph, five minutes later, slowly entered the boys' loos.
(And prayed no baddies lurked there that could make
him headline news!)
He walked into one cubicle and quickly shut the door,
Then sat in contemplation with his eyes fixed on the floor.

And then a gloved hand pushed a note that slid between
Ralph's feet,
A message clearly written on a toilet-paper sheet:
'Trust no-one, Ralph, and CERTAINLY not troublesome
Jean-Claude,
I've gathered lots of evidence which proves that he's a fraud!'

"Who ARE you?" Ralph then scribbled back. 'A FRIEND,'
a note replied.

(This message on a fresh sheet – Ralph had used the other side.)
'It's true The Chess Academy have planned a kidnap plot,
But Jean-Claude is INVOLVED, Ralph – yes, he's done this
quite a lot!'

"Er, do I know you?" Ralph wrote back.
'YOU DO,' the next note stated.
'Just like you, Ralph, I think being cool is over-rated!
We can't talk here – the walls have ears – the paper's running out.
Just meet me in the park at four, I'll answer any doubt!'

One final note arrived and Ralph heard footsteps walk away.
'There's one important thing left that I think I ought to say:
You must dispose of all these notes – the method's up to you,
But (just to play it safe) may I suggest a number two?'

MISSION-OGRAM

YOU MUST INVENT YOUR OWN
SPY ALIAS. STOP.

WHAT IS YOUR UNDERCOVER SPY
NAME? STOP.

INVENT YOUR PRETEND JOB/
ADDRESS/ FAMILY. END.

CHAPTER 4

JAWS!

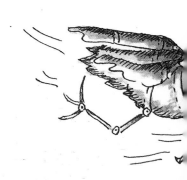

Ralph's sister said, 'Jean-Claude and I are walking
home tonight –
I don't want you to bother us, so please stay out of sight!
We're going to the fun fair first, but we'll be home for dinner.'
(The fair that had arrived in town was proving quite a winner!)

"Just go for it!" said Ralph. "Besides, I've plans for after school."
'Don't tell me . . . playing chess?' sis said.
'Or something else un-cool?'
"Well, thanks for your concern, but please don't worry –
I'll be fine . . .
You just mind your own business, sis,
and leave me to mind mine!"

Ralph rolled up to the park, then found an empty bench
and waited,
Whilst thinking all this spy-stuff was becoming over-rated!
He glanced around – but didn't see a stranger had now sat
Directly down beside him, in a matching mac and hat!

'Hello, Ralph . . . Please don't look at me –
keep looking straight ahead.
To let me know you understand, just nod or shake your head.
I've watched you now for many months and often wondered why
Someone so wise and cunning shouldn't also be a spy?

Let's face it, Ralph, you've got the brains, the uniform . . .
and mac.
May I assume you're armed if there's an enemy attack?'
"Armed with what?" Ralph panicked. "I've no weapon . . .
I've no gun!"
(Revising his opinion that a spy's life might be fun!)

'But surely that is why your mac is out-size, like my own?
Concealing all our gadgets . . . weapons . . . handcuffs . . .
mobile phone?'
"Er . . . sadly not," Ralph answered. "It's a little large – that's true.
My mum just buys things BIG, so they will last a year or two!"

'Well, let's get down to business – there's a plot to take your sis.'
"Excuse me," Ralph replied, "but I've already heard all this.
The Chess Academy are so resentful of my skill,
That they intend both me (and her) a gesture of ill-will!

My question now is this – you may have gadgets up your sleeve
But Jean-Claude says that HE'S the spy –
so who should I believe?
I've no idea who YOU are . . . and HE'S a stranger too . . .
So who's the REAL spy here – is it HIM or is it YOU?"

'I understand your point, Ralph,
and you're someone that I trust
Against all spying regulations, I can see I must
Confide in you – believe in ME and you will not be conned
With any lies or falsehoods . . . I'm your classmate –
Blair McBond!'

"Blair? . . . It's you? . . . The quiet one? . . . Even quieter than me?"
'That's WHY I keep my profile and my presence so low-key . . .
And I don't work alone . . .' said Blair
(cue long dramatic pause)
'. . . but with our new class mascot: yes, the gerbil,
name of Jaws[1]!

---

[1] See Spy Zone page 84 to discover what Jaws has written in code!

By day Jaws just pretends to be your average furry pet,
But this, my friend, will shock you more than all the rest,
I'll bet.
The minute that he has some information to off-load
He lets me know by tapping out the message . . .
in MORSE[2] CODE!

And every day, or night, when there's a mission we must face
I substitute this model of a gerbil in his place.
He travels in my pocket and it's handy he's so small . . .
I've yet to find a space that's too confined for him to crawl!'

"Well, that explains a lot!" Ralph said. "In fact, I've overheard
Strange rattlings in code and was becoming quite a-feared . . .
That I was going mad!" 'NO, NOT AT ALL!' was Blair's reply.
'You see – I wasn't wrong, Ralph.
Yes – ALREADY you're a spy!'

---

[2] See Spy Zone page 82 to find out about Morse code.

"Me? . . . A SPY? . . . I THINK NOT, BLAIR! . . .
But have you ever seen . . .
A bird quite like that pink one there in *Bird Life* magazine?
It hasn't moved, or made a sound, the whole time what we've talked
And even when that cat passed by, it neither flinched nor squawked!"

'ABORT! ABORT! Ralph – you're correct –
you see, YOU ARE A SPY!
My guard was down – there's no excuse –
that bird will NEVER fly!
Inspect its left leg closely – see the sound bug on its claw?
The camera hidden in its beak? Ralph . . . RUN AND SAY
NO MORE!'

But many, many miles away, a darkened figure winced:
'Who IS this pesky guttersnipe?
I'm growing quite convinced . . .
That we have underestimated Ralph and this . . . McBond.
They are a clever pair of whom I'm growing MOST un-fond!'

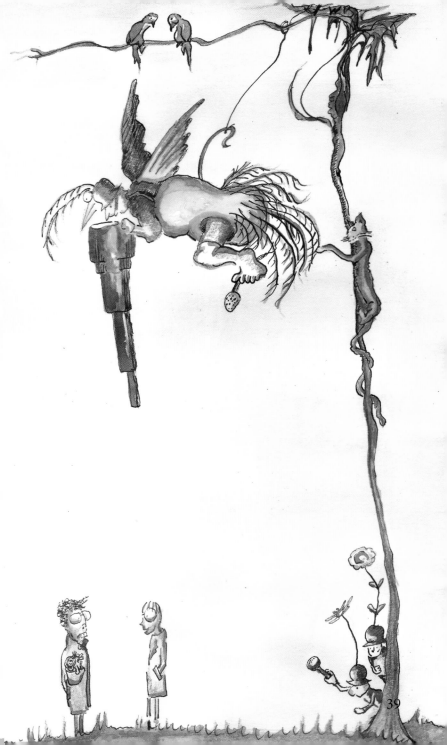

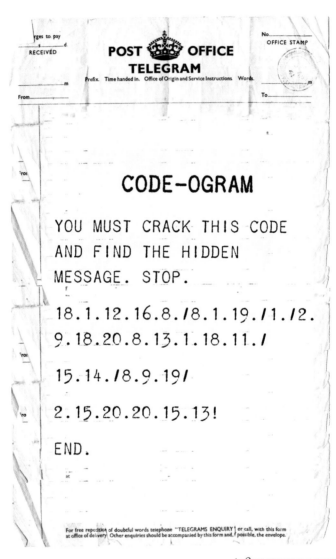

CODE-OGRAM

YOU MUST CRACK THIS CODE
AND FIND THE HIDDEN
MESSAGE. STOP.

18.1.12.16.8./8.1.19./1./2.
9.18.20.8.13.1.18.11./

15.14./8.9.19/

2.15.20.20.15.13!

END.

For free repetition of doubtful words telephone "TELEGRAMS ENQUIRY" or call, with this form
at office of delivery Other enquiries should be accompanied by this form and, if possible, the envelope.

CHAPTER 5

KNIGHT! KNIGHT!

Ralph staggered home, bewildered,
as he tried to think it through.
Already, in his heart of hearts, he felt he really knew
That Blair McBond had always been a silent, decent chap.
And so it must be true: Jean-Claude was sent to lay a trap!

Ralph missed his girlfriend, Amy, who by now was
feeling better . . .
Her 'flu was nearly over (she'd assured him in a letter),
And said perhaps she'd visit him that day, straight after school,
For she was finding all this spy talk really rather cool!

But, sadly, when poor Ralph had reached his house
at half-past four
He found a note from Amy – she could visit him no more.
Jean-Claude had 'warned her off' it said. 'And, for at least a week,
"Security restrictions" meant the two must NEVER speak.'

Apparently she'd popped in to see Ralph the day before.
(Quite unaware, of course, of what her visit held in store!)
Jean-Claude had hypnotised her –
then he'd questioned her at length
On all Ralph's hidden secrets . . . every weakness . . .
every strength.

With that the front door opened and Jean-Claude

(and sis) appeared.

'You feeling OK, Ralph?' she said. 'You're looking REALLY weird!'

"I'm quite well," he responded as he hurried through the hall . . .

Then dashed upstairs to secretly give Amy a quick call.

"That's right – the good guy's Blair McBond!"

Ralph spoke in muted tone . . .

To Amy, from the attic, on his mother's mobile phone.

"I fear the landline may be bugged, so get me on this line.

But please don't worry – I'll be safe – with Blair I'll be just fine!"

'You're scaring me!' said Amy. 'Please, Ralph, don't take

ANY chances.

You must report it all to Blair – all whispers, sideways glances . . .

Or anything you think may be suspicious in the least.

We must defeat Jean-Claude: that cruel (but pleasant-

smelling) beast!

He said that I was EVIL, Ralph – he claimed he knew I planned,

To contaminate you all with 'flu – he's getting out of hand!'

"Check ALL your clothes . . . and tissues, Amy – he'll have

bugged you too . . .

I even found one sound bug on the cistern of our loo!"

The next day, back at school, poor Ralph became a bit confused,
When an urgent call of nature meant Blair asked to be excused.
Ralph heard a violent tapping – then saw, up on his back paws,
Busy banging out a message was a most disgruntled[1] . . . Jaws!

'RALPH, I'VE HEARD YOU KNOW MORSE CODE –
SO IF THAT'S REALLY TRUE
THEN PASS THIS MESSAGE TO MCBOND,
IT'S VITAL THAT YOU DO:
**"PREPARE THE HORSES AND PREPARE
THE 99S AS WELL."**
I INTERCEPTED THIS –
BUT WHAT IT'S CODE FOR, WHO CAN TELL?'

---

[1] See Spy Zone page 92.

Ralph scribbled it down quickly, hoping Jean-Claude
hadn't seen
Then deftly slid the note inside his *Chess Champs* magazine.
Then, as they left the class, he passed the magazine to Blair
Whilst giving him a secret wink and knowledgeable stare.

Then, early afternoon, Ralph had his *favourite* class: PE,
But as he put his gym shoes on, was most surprised to see . . .
A message had been written on both soles, which simply read:
'Meet me once again at four – the OTHER bench instead.'

'You see? . . . You ARE a spy, my friend,' Blair said to Ralph, at four.
'You're BRILLIANT for someone who has not done this before!
I've checked each bird, each twig, for bugs – but this time we
are fine.
I even checked the clothing on that neighbouring washing line!'

45

Right now, your sister and Jean-Claude are at the ice-cream van,
You MUST accept this mission, Ralph – and do the best you can!
And when you have succeeded, here's the number you
must phone:
Your mission is to get the prints from Jean-Claude's
ice-cream cone.

GO NOW! There is no time to lose! Good luck!' McBond departed.
Ralph gathered all his things up . . . took a nervous gulp,
then darted
Towards the ice-cream van – and found his sister and Jean-Claude
Both chatting, holding 99s (though J-C looked quite bored!).

"Oh, hiyah, sis!" Ralph started. "Gosh, those ice creams
look SO good.

Jean-Claude, you're NEARLY finished, though –
I wonder if could . . .

Beg one small favour . . . do you think that it would be all right,
If I requested that you leave me just a single bite?"

'*Mais bien sûr!*' Jean-Claude exclaimed.
'I'll buy one – just for you.'

"No, really!" Ralph replied. "Please – just your FINAL bite
will do.

I've not too big an appetite, so that will just suffice.
I know it's quite an odd request, but ONE bite would be nice!"

He handed Ralph the piece of cone, as sis began to say,

'Yes, Ralph, it is official – you grow weirder every day!'

Big sis and Jean-Claude then took off. When they were
out of view

Ralph quickly phoned the number, as McBond had said to do.

'Well done,' Blair said. 'Now meet me in the library in ten.

The cone is vital evidence – I'll prove it to you then.'

Ralph found him in the archives and the cone was
then exchanged.

Then tests were run . . . 'EUREKA!' shouted Blair
(a bit deranged).

'I had suspicions all along – but here is proof indeed.

I knew that finger-print results were all that I would need,

To prove beyond a doubt what I suspected all too well . . .

Jean-Claude? He comes from Bolton and his real name's
Ivor Smell!

You see . . .' McBond continued '. . . he first gave himself away

By using all that aftershave which, Ralph, I have to say

He uses to disguise the fact he's really rather smelly . . .

You may have seen him talked about on *Crimewatch* on the telly!'

'Drat . . . and drat . . . and DOUBLE DRAT!'

a voice began to say . . .

In a dark and secret bunker many hundred miles away.

(Poor Ralph had checked his clothing – even checked between his toes,

But as he slept, Jean-Claude had placed a sound bug up Ralph's nose!)

'They're on to us! . . . THEY'RE ON TO US!'

the bony figure cried.

'They know who Ivor REALLY is. So, friends, we must decide

To bring our mission forward, as I know beyond a doubt,

Although they're good – they'll NEVER work our evil mission out!'

Meanwhile, McBond said, 'Ralph – go home.

Don't hint at what you've learned . . .

Act NORMAL when you're near him –

soon his fingers will get burned!'

But when Ralph reached his bedroom,

he received the biggest fright:

As pinned upon his pillow was a warning note:

'KNIGHT! KNIGHT!'

POST OFFICE
TELEGRAM

MISSION-OGRAM

DESIGN YOUR OWN ESSENTIAL
SPY KIT. STOP.

DECIDE WHAT YOU REALLY NEED
ON ALL MISSIONS. STOP.

DON'T FORGET YOUR CHEESE
SANDWICH. END.

CHAPTER 6

THE WHIFFY HOSTAGE

'A THREAT!' McBond replied,
once Ralph had phoned him with the news.
'Their plans must be in place and so we've little
time to lose!
Let's meet at four tomorrow – at the fun fair, if you can . . .
Together, Ralph, we HAVE to thwart their evil kidnap plan!'

Ralph tossed and turned all night, as he lay sweating in his bed,
With clues and ghastly visions busy floating round his head.
Then saw a text on Jean-Claude's phone and knew what
it must mean:
'The pawns are in position and are soon to seize the Queen.'

The next day, Ralph was early for his meeting at the fair.
He went to find a drinks stall as he had some time to spare,
But paying for his apple juice, he quickly overheard . . .
'I'll have the same as Ralph, but like mine *shaken* and not *stirred*.'

"McBond," Ralph whispered quietly –
though no one was around.
He looked for clues and quickly saw
the droppings on the ground.

The gerbil droppings made a trail,
which Ralph was pleased to see
Would lead him straight
to Blair (and Jaws)
behind the
biggest tree.

53

'Be careful, Ralph – we're being watched, more closely than you'd think!'

(As Blair removed a sound bug from his 'shaken' apple drink.)

'Let's piece the clues together – but keep watch for hidden spies . . .'

While Jaws continued tapping out,

'BEWARE THE HORSE THAT FLIES![1]'

'And so, Ralph, now the time has come, although you might have guessed . . .

Just some of what this plot entails – we MUST work out the rest!'

"NO NEED!" Ralph cried. "My goodness, Blair, it's OBVIOUS of course:

Their evil plot revolves around some ice cream . . . and a horse!

Glance over there: the carousel man, with the evil eyes . . .

That he's involved in this, well, it should come as no surprise!

You see the lilac horse named 'Parta' – Blair, feel free to clap . . .

I've just worked out that 'PARTA' backwards really spells 'A TRAP'.

And, to your left: the ice-cream van – or so they'd have us think,

But any van inspector would report it in a blink!

They only sell a 99 . . . no lollies, juice or sweets . . .

The driver's always very rude to everyone he meets!

---

[1] See Spy Zone page 84 to double-check Jaws's message yourself!

So Jean-Claude brings my sister here each single day from school,
Of course she hasn't realised he's played her for a fool!
He makes her ride his *favourite* horse . . . named PARTA . . . after that
They go and buy a 99 and have a lovely chat!

It's really quite ingenious – all the details are in place . . .
The carousel and ice-cream man both recognise her face.
Then as she rides they'll speed the carousel up – really fast –
And execute their evil plan to kidnap her at last.

For as her fellow riders all feel dizzy and quite sick
(This part though, Blair, I must admit, I think is rather slick),
They'll press the special button, which will open a trapdoor . . .
My sister will then disappear beneath the wooden floor.

And underneath the floor, they've built a tunnel to the van.
The ice-cream man will grab her – then return as quick he can,
Before the decoy raises the alarm: 'She's disappeared!'
The van could be five miles away, precisely as we feared."

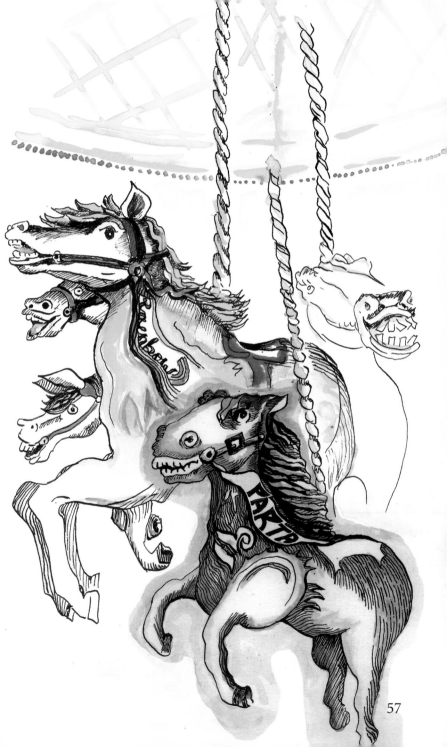

57

'My goodness, Ralph, though I've been in this spying game
for years,
The DETAILS of this kidnap plot have brought me close to tears!
I couldn't work the last part out, yet YOU could, which is why . . .
I'm going to ask you once again: You're sure you're not a spy?'

"It's genius," said Ralph. "They've given this a lot of time . . .
There must be simpler ways for them to execute this crime!"
'The Chess Academy . . .' said Blair '. . . are such a stylish crew.
To steal your playing secrets, there is NOTHING they won't do!

But still we don't know WHEN they plan to carry out this plot.
I need to question Jean-Claude NOW . . . he must confess the lot!
We'll need some reinforcements – and some stand-by
transport too . . .
Your mum and dad both drive a car, so either one will do!'

"But, Blair, how can we bring him in for questioning?"
Ralph began.
"He's bound to be suspicious that we're working out their plan."
'You are correct, my friend,' Blair said. 'It's sorted –
please don't fret!
Last night I looked up *sleeping potions* . . . on the internet!

I've sent for the ingredients – though some were hard to source:
(Some plants we'll need grow only in the Amazon, of course!)
It might take several days, although I paid for Express Post.
We'll have to hope and pray by then your sister isn't toast!'

Ralph said, "Remember Kurt at school? He's great at science,
you know?
He spends weekends and evenings with his test-tubes all a-glow!
Kurt MUST know how to make that sleeping gas you see
on telly . . .
The one they use in hospitals that turns your legs to jelly!

We replace Jean-Claude's hair spray with this gas to knock
him out,
Then seize him early morning, when there's nobody about . . .
And carry him to somewhere quiet where no-one passes by
THEN we interrogate him . . . Blair, it must be worth a try?"

'Ralph – I like your style! That's simply *brilliant*!' Blair began.
'He never would suspect we'd tamper with his hair-spray can!
At first I really thought a sleeping potion would be slicker,
But knowing time's against us, Ralph – well, YOUR way
would be quicker!'

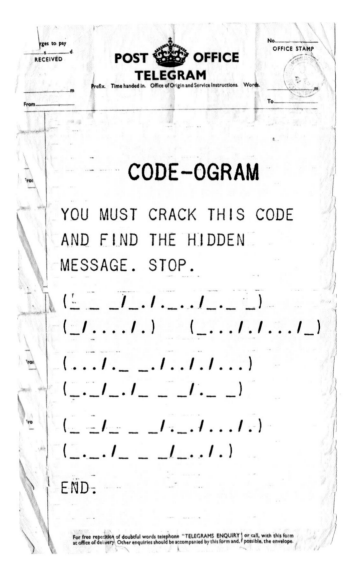

CODE-OGRAM

YOU MUST CRACK THIS CODE
AND FIND THE HIDDEN
MESSAGE. STOP.

(_ _ _/_./._../_._ _)
(_/...../.)   (_.../././_)
(.../._ _./../././...)
(._/_./_ _ _/._ _)
(_ _/_ _ _/._./..../.)
(_._./_ _ _/_../.)

END.

For free repetition of doubtful words telephone "TELEGRAMS ENQUIRY" or call, with this form at office of delivery Other enquiries should be accompanied by this form and, f possible, the envelope.

(Solution: Look up the Morse code guide on page 83 of The Spy Zone and then work out Ralph's secret message!)
Only the best spies know Morse code.

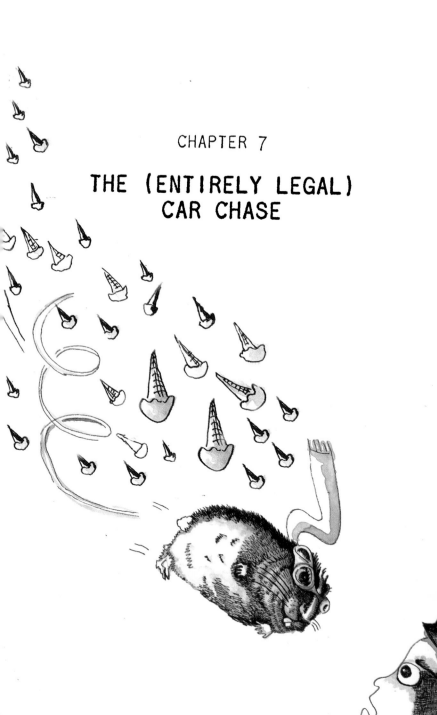

CHAPTER 7

THE (ENTIRELY LEGAL) CAR CHASE

'You brought me here?' Jean-Claude began,
his blindfold once removed.
'I must admit, I'm quite surprised the library
staff approved!
I would have picked an old abandoned tenement myself . . .'
Then turned and found his left hand firmly handcuffed
to a shelf!

McBond just smirked, then chose a book.
'Look – *Fish: Their Likes and Fears.*
I think you'll find these books have not been touched for
many years!
Take this one here: last borrowed, yes . . . in 1892!
I don't suppose there'll be too many passers-by . . . DO YOU?

So let's begin, Jean-Claude, or should I call you **Ivor Smell**?
I've tracked you over many weeks, so feel I know you well!
We know to take Ralph's sister is your current kidnap plan . . .
But be advised – I've set a trap on board the ice-cream van!

Ralph, open up his briefcase, combination 1, 2, 3.
Just take the briefest look inside and tell me what you see . . .
No proper agent goes to work when he has lives to save
Armed purely with a hairspray and some pungent aftershave!

Pathetic! . . . Where's his sandwich? . . . Or his spy glass? . . .
Or his mac?

Only the very WORST of spies would not know what to pack!

He's certainly not French, Ralph, and his hair is not that big . . .

For give it just the slightest tug – it's actually a wig!'

'What do you want from me?' poor Ivor stammered with a cry.

'WHEN do you plan to take her?' the immediate reply.

'And just in case you're not convinced you really should
confess . . .

Ralph will begin explaining all his FAVOURITE moves
in chess!'

'Nooooo!' poor Ivor bellowed. 'I've no pencil! Stop him, PLEASE!
I MUSTN'T talk . . . I CAN'T!' he stuttered, falling to his knees.
'I thought that's what you'd say!' McBond replied,
with ghoulish smirk.
'Gives me the chance to see if my new gadget here will work . . .'

McBond produced a second case, then quickly reached inside.
"What's THAT?" asked Ralph. 'Observe my NEW invention!'
Blair replied.
'I call it my "*Truth Helmet*" . . . which, when placed upon
the head
Will block out any lies – you're forced to tell the truth instead!'

'It won't work . . . I WON'T TELL YOU!'

Jean-Claude whispered petrified.

But once placed in the helmet, he soon started to confide:

'I was supposed to meet her at the carousel today

At 5 o'clock – she'll be there now – you'd best be on your way!'

And many miles away, the darkened figure gave a wail:

'IVOR – YOU'RE AN IDIOT! . . . Our plan just CANNOT fail!

Your vanity has nearly stopped us acting out this crime.

My only consolation is – they're running out of time!'

The two boys fled and found Ralph's mum with Amy in the car.

'JUST DRIVE!' McBond commanded. 'Now they've taken
this too far!'

"Head for the fun fair, Mum," Ralph said, "it's just next to our school."

'And put your foot down!' Amy yelled. 'A CAR CHASE . . .

THIS IS COOL!'

'We're late!' (McBond was sweating.)

'But I've still one card to play.

I broke into the ice-cream van in question yesterday . . .

And rigged their music siren, so it's constantly on LOUD.

We'll hear them and we'll follow them!' he added, feeling proud.

'BE QUIET! I HEAR MUSIC!'

Jaws was tapping on his cage.

'He's right, I hear some nursery rhymes – just faintly at this stage.

You've got to put your foot down NOW!' McBond began to plead.

'Now, boys . . .' replied Ralph's mum. 'A speeding fine is all we need!

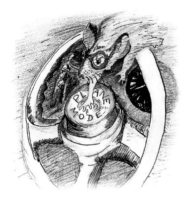

For if you check the signs, then
you will all be sure to see:
The twenty miles per hour zone
that we're stuck in presently.

I'm keen to reach your sister
– I can see the van ahead –
But I will NEVER break
the law!' Ralph's mother
curtly[1] said.

'I hear them! . . . Look, they're still in sight! Keep going!'
Amy cried.
'With all that music blaring, there's no place for them to hide!'
But suddenly, from nowhere, any hope had disappeared
As Ruth stepped out in front of them, just as McBond had feared!

The children all crossed quietly, but Ruth remained quite still.
'She's nodded off!' Ralph's mum explained. 'She didn't take
her pill!'

---

[1] See Spy Zone page 92.

'MOVE!' McBond commanded. 'This is really not the place
For Ruth to fall asleep – we're in a rather crucial race!'

'I can't go round! . . . There's just no room! . . .
WE'RE DOOMED!' Ralph's mum began,
The four of them all listening to the distant ice-cream van.
'Don't despair!' Blair shouted. 'As I've rigged your mum's car too
And if you press that button, you'll see just what it can do!'

Ralph pressed the big red
button and the car began
to creak
Then slowly rose into the
air. (His mum could barely
speak.)

'IT'S STILTS . . . THE CAR'S
ON STILTS!' cried Amy,
with bewildered stare,
While safely driving 'over'
Ruth from miles up in the air.

69

"They're pelting us with missiles now! THEY'RE ARMED!"
poor Ralph began,
As ice-cream cones were hurled out from the speeding
ice-cream van.
"It's made the road too slippy – it's the last thing that we need.
In such icy conditions Mum must FURTHER drop her speed!"

'ABORT! ABORT THE MISSION! WE'RE NO LONGER
SAFE!' Blair cried.
'We can't risk any casualties . . . just let them go,' he sighed.
'Let's just return to base and then we'll do the best we can
To try to salvage something from our bungled rescue plan!'

'First up, call the police!' McBond began, arriving back.
'We'll need more reinforcements now to plan our new attack!'
But entering the kitchen first, Blair yelled, 'HOW CAN THIS BE?'
As Ralph came running down the hall and shouted: "Let ME see!"

He stopped to switch the light on, as he ran in after Blair.
His sis was sitting tied and gagged upon a kitchen chair!
And stapled (rather crudely) to her new expensive sweater
The baddies had attempted to explain things in a letter . . .

MISSION–OGRAM

YOU MUST IDENTIFY THE
SECRET SPY IN YOUR CLASS.
STOP.

IS IT A QUIETER CLASS
MEMBER OR EVEN THE TEACHER?
STOP.

WRITE A STORY ABOUT YOUR
ADVENTURES WITH YOUR SPY
FRIEND. END.

CHAPTER 8

JAWS EXPLAINS IT ALL

'Just WHAT is going on?' Ralph's dad had entered,
quite confused.
'If this has all been just some joke . . .
I'm really not amused!
I got your message, called the police and quickly hurried home . . .
Although you all know, speeding's not a thing we can condone!'[1]

'I've suffered! HOW I've suffered!' Ralph's sis earnestly began.
'I'm still so shocked and weary – but I'll tell you what I can!
Their manners were appalling,
and some members were quite smelly.
I asked for caviar, but got a cup of soup and jelly!

I thought they planned to KILL me,
or do something WORSE than that . . .
As yesterday I had this lovely manicure – with Pat.
They knew my nails would be my pride and joy,
so thought it better
To torture me by CUTTING one to send with ransom letter!'

---

[1] See Spy Zone page 92.

'It seems,' McBond began,

'they bit off more than they could chew . . .

They took her, but within the hour have brought her back to you!

Her whining and her big demands were driving them insane,

Of all the folk they've kidnapped, she's by far the biggest pain!'

With that, his mobile phone rang –

Ralph's dad picked it up a-pace

'That's great!' he said. 'I'll tell McBond that he can close the case.

The police soon heard the van and caught it only streets away

All thanks to Blair ensuring it belts music night and day!'

They all retired for tea and cakes and mused[2] about their day,

McBond insisted Ralph had had a MAJOR part to play!

'And yet, I hate to be a party pooper . . .' started Blair

'. . . but think you'll find Ralph's sister is still tied up

to that chair!'

Five hours later, once big sis had thrice re-lived her story

She finally retired to bed to dream of captive glory.

'I should be off,' McBond began. 'I'm glad I could assist.

But if you're asked if I was here – the truth you must resist!'

---

[2] See Spy Zone page 92.

"I don't know how you do it, Blair, I never would have guessed
You've got these hidden talents that you hide from all the rest!
How can you take the teasing, when you know that deep inside
You live a life of danger that you're always forced to hide?"

'With all your brains and wisdom,
Ralph, you really haven't heard?
The last to rouse suspicion is the clever, silent nerd!
To others my life's boring, but we both know they're
quite wrong . . .
It lets me do my job in peace – if I just play along!

The truth is this: you'll find a spy in every class at school . . .
The quiet one – like you, or me – that others brand "un-cool".
In fact we're just too busy eyeing up suspicious cases
Which might appear at any time (in most unusual places)!

But promise me this one thing, Ralph?
From now on you will be
Aware of all the secret lives of comrades just like me.
If others want to think us dull – well, let them think it's true
For they would die of shock if they knew HALF of what we do!'

HOW TO DO A SECRET HANDSHAKE

STEP 1: 'NORMAL' SHAKE

STEP 2: BUT HIDDEN 2 FINGER PRESS ON UNDERSIDE

STEP 3: QUICK GRIP

STEP 4: LIGHT FINGER 'WIBBLE' AT END.

Blair gave his secret handshake, then he turned to leave at speed.
'Remember, Ralph, you're just the sort of chap we'll ALWAYS need.
You know where you can find me, if you ever change your mind
And want to join my agency – you're just the *spying kind*!'

The next day, back at school, Ralph's sis enjoyed all the attention
(Though talking through the lessons quickly earned her
a detention!).
She asked the Drama Club if they would stage a new
production . . .
About her brush with criminals and (very brief) abduction!

And many, many miles away, a darkened figure cried:
'WE FAILED! WE'VE BEEN OUTSMARTED!
IT'S AN INSULT TO OUR PRIDE!
Yet we must try again to learn the secret of Ralph's game . . .
Though next time we'll NOT send my son,
as HE'S the one to blame!'

But spare a thought for Ivor, as he started to compute . . .
Whilst held within his local 'Young Offenders Institute'.
This place held no cosmetics: hair spray, wigs or aftershave . . .
Plus he was forced to share with two large smelly chaps
named Dave.

Back in Ralph's school, things had returned
to normal straight away.
McBond and he were picked on – which was an average day.
Ralph turned to Blair and muttered, as he gave a secret wink,
"We know the truth now, comrade, so WHO CARES what
they all think?"

Then, as the lesson started, both boys heard a tapping noise,
Beneath the chattering voices of the other girls and boys.
'REMEMBER, FOLKS,' Jaws added. 'THINGS AREN'T
ALWAYS WHAT THEY SEEM . . .
BEWARE THE SUAVE BUT SMELLY[3] . . .
KEEP THE QUIET ONES ON YOUR TEAM!'

THE END

---

[3] See Spy Zone page 84 to work out your final message from Jaws!

SPY ZONE

Now, before you fully enter the Spy Zone . . . take a good look over your shoulder. Were you followed? Are you being watched? Have you checked your clothing for hidden sound bugs? Only continue reading when you are ABSOLUTELY SURE there are no enemy eyes upon you . . . Really? . . . Nobody at all? . . . What about him over there? . . . You're sure? . . . Oh, OK, carry on then . . .

WELCOME TO THE SPY ZONE!

Here you will find an assortment of further spy activities and missions for you to accept, but they are not for the faint-hearted. There are another fifty ⭐ **Spy Stars** ⭐ up for grabs in this section. Proceed with caution and accept each mission . . . ONLY IF YOU DARE!

Let's start at the top . . . all spies (just like Ralph and Blair) need to converse in code and the most famous code in the world is:

MORSE CODE

Morse code was invented by Samuel F. B. Morse, who died in 1872, so it has been around EVEN LONGER than Ralph's sister! The first Morse code message ever was sent from Washington to Baltimore in America. Experienced spies don't need to write anything down, but can converse at 20-30 words per minute (a long sound beat or flash of light means a dash and a short sound or flash means a dot) . . . that's pretty fast! A lot of people know it best as something used as a distress or 'HELP' signal, so usually they will hear taps or see flashes of light signalling (. . . _ _ _ . . .) or S.O.S., which means 'Save our Souls' or 'HELP!' and is often used by ships at sea. Why not try tapping it out? Tap quickly for a dot and more slowly for a dash.

All good spies should know how to use this, so here's your very own guide to the code. (You must of course eat this page once you have learned it, to prevent it falling into enemy hands!) Why not try flashing out a simple message by torchlight (using quick flashes for dots and longer flashes for dashes) or tapping it out with shorter and longer beats? Award yourself one **Spy Star** for every message you learn, or a maximum five **Spy Stars** once you are fluent! Why not just start by working out your phone number in Morse code?

A	.—	N	—.	0	— — — — —
B	—...	O	— — —	1	.— — — —
C	—.—.	P	.— —.	2	..— — —
D	—..	Q	— —.—	3	...— —
E	.	R	.—.	4	....—
F	..—.	S	...	5	.....
G	— —.	T	—	6	—....
H	....	U	..—	7	— — ...
I	..	V	...—	8	— — —..
J	.— — —	W	.— —	9	— — — —.
K	—.—	X	—..—		
L	.—..	Y	—.— —		
M	— —	Z	— —..		

Do you remember Jaws tapping out messages in Morse during exciting episodes in the book? Here they are again, so use the table above to help translate them. Award yourself one **Spy Star** for each message you translate. Answers below!

Look again at Jaws's coded message on p. 34.

(----/--/---/---) (--/---) (-/----/-) (--/--/---/-) . (---/----/----/--/--/---)
(--/---) (-/----/-) (---/--/--/-)

Look again at Jaws's coded message on p. 53.

(----/-/---/--/---/-) (-/----/-) (----/---/--/----/-) (-/----/--/-) (---/----/--/-/---)

Look again at Jaws's coded message at the very end of the story on p. 80.

(--/-/-/----/-/-/---) (-/---/---/---/-) (---/--/-/-/----/----/----) (---/---/-/----/---)

(On p. 34 Jaws is actually saying: 'Jaws is the name. Spying is the game.' On p. 53 Jaws is actually saying: 'Beware the horse that flies.' On p. 80 Jaws is actually saying: 'Never trust smelly folk.')

•   •   •   •   •

How is it going so far? Anything suspicious to report? Have you been rumbled as a code-breaker yet? Remember, TRUST NOBODY! . . . Particularly not that bloke in the dark glasses standing behind you . . . ha ha, made you look! Best move on quickly to the next section . . .

STRESSFUL SPY SCENARIOS!

Every good spy has to think on their feet and make split-second decisions . . . COULD YOU? Take a look at the following five scenarios that all international spies could find themselves in at any moment. You have only seconds to decide what to do . . . people are counting on you! Award yourself a **Spy Star** for every situation you think of a solution to (within a 10-SECOND time limit) . . . READY? . . . **GO!**

You are tracking a suspect, Luke S. Dodgy, through the streets of a city during a busy festival. There are street entertainers, noises and people crowded everywhere. Your suspect joins the crowd watching a fire-eating act, then pulls out his mobile phone to make a call. You really need to overhear what the suspect says, but the fire-eater has asked you to help him out with his next trick. You mustn't arouse suspicion . . . **WHAT DO YOU DO?**

You are in France for the international ice-dancing championships. You find the changing room for the British candidate, Therma L. Drawers, as you have been reliably informed that an evil spy has 'tampered' with her ice-skates, so that they will be out of control and make her fall. When you enter, she is already wearing the skates and is about to head to the side of the ring for her routine. The cameras are rolling . . . **WHAT DO YOU DO?**

The Head of the famous RRSB (Ridiculously Rich Savings Bank) has requested your services. They have a wealthy investor coming for a meeting at 1 p.m., but when you arrive in good time to carry out your security checks in advance, you are informed he arrived two hours early with his own security guards and is already in a meeting with the Head. When you check back on the CCTV footage, he looks suspiciously like international bank robber Lotso Dosh, so you must get into that room immediately. Who do you say you are, so as not to arouse suspicion, and then . . . **WHAT DO YOU DO?**

Marinus Fishby, the well-known evil marine biologist, has been terrorising local swimming pools by threatening to release his pet baby shark during their busy Children's Hours. There are inflatable slides and giant inflatable octopuses that could be punctured, let alone an array of young children swimming with armbands who could be left stranded – or worse! You've tracked Marinus and know he is already in the building. As you glance around, you see that many children have their own inflatable toy sharks with them too, so you must identify the correct shark and somehow capture it without terrorising the swimmers . . . **WHAT DO YOU DO?**

Your local vicar is about to judge the Parish Cheekiest Chutney Competition when he is struck down by a sudden attack of heartburn. You are observing as you have intercepted the news that Abundance O'Chilli (internationally renowned for his competition offerings, which are always over-spiced . . . and occasionally poisoned) is in attendance. The vicar's wife spies you in the audience and asks if you can take over the judging by tasting all the entries. Remember, all the entrants are in the audience so you mustn't arouse suspicion or cause any offence . . . **WHAT DO YOU DO?**

FURTHER SPY MISSIONS

Now you're really getting the hang of this spying thing, what a natural! Why not try a few more missions to test your natural spying abilities further? Remember, award yourself a **Spy Star** *for every mission you complete! Oh, and by the way . . . HE'S STILL BEHIND YOU!*

Why not . . .

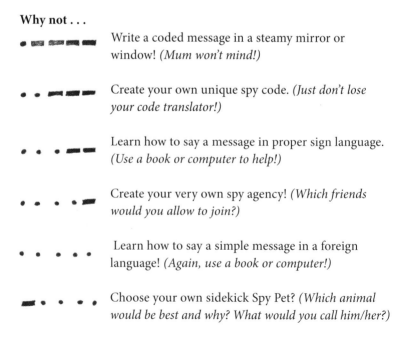

Write a coded message in a steamy mirror or window! *(Mum won't mind!)*

Create your own unique spy code. *(Just don't lose your code translator!)*

Learn how to say a message in proper sign language. *(Use a book or computer to help!)*

Create your very own spy agency! *(Which friends would you allow to join?)*

Learn how to say a simple message in a foreign language! *(Again, use a book or computer!)*

Choose your own sidekick Spy Pet? *(Which animal would be best and why? What would you call him/her?)*

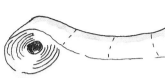

Or why not . . . cut a very long strip of paper, about 2cm wide . . .

. . . wind it around an empty toilet roll and write a message across the coiled paper? When it is unravelled, only fellow spies who know about the toilet-paper code will re-wind it and read the whole message. To everyone else it looks like useless random words!

Or why not . . . try making your own invisible ink?

Use lemon juice/milk to write an invisible message on a sheet of paper and apply a heat/light source (a hair dryer or high-voltage light bulb) to see the message magically appear before your eyes!

Or why not try making your own spy gadgets?

You could make simple walkie-talkies, or something more complicated like a magnifying glass or periscope. (Very useful for seeing over taller people's heads while on a mission!) There are lots of ideas on the internet, so ask an adult or teacher to help you find some simple instructions.

Let's move on and not mention that peculiar-looking blackbird with binoculars staring at you from the window sill. I know . . . you've probably already clocked it! Now, all spies need to be multi-talented so let's see how you are at drawing . . .

SPY—ART

Why not try to draw:

• Yourself in your own chosen spy disguise? *(Are you absolutely sure you won't be recognised?)*

• Draw your teacher/family members in disguise? *(Who would make the worst or best spy, do you think?)*

• Design your own spy alias ID?

• Draw your chosen ultimate spy gadget? *(Complete with instructions on how each bit works, or any hidden compartments.)*

• Create your own code with a series of picture messages?

For example:

 means . . . I CAN SEE YOU!!

Award yourself one **Spy Star** for each of the five missions you complete!

•　　•　　•　　•　　•

I'm not even going to mention that five-legged cat sitting over there in your dad's prize oak tree. I'm sure you know all about it! Now, sometimes, on missions, all spies have to do surprisingly ordinary things like take a bus or even buy a sandwich. Even then, you must keep your wits about you. For example, would you recognise a fake coin or banknote?

COUNTERFEIT MONEY!

All good spies should always be on the look-out for fake or counterfeit money. You might be paid in fake notes for a spy mission you perform, or you might witness someone using fake money to buy an expensive painting or jewel. How can you tell it's a fake?

Many businesses and banks use special machines and pens to tell if a bank note is genuine or fake. The special machines will shine ultraviolet light on to the note and if it is genuine its value will appear in bright red or green letters. However, for those of us without a machine, there are many websites (like lovemoney.com) which tell us there are some checks we can make for ourselves, looking for obvious clues!

 When you hold the note up to the light you can see an image of the queen's portrait, but you shouldn't be able to see the watermark when the note is lying flat.

Fake notes feel less like smooth cloth and far more like rough paper.

There should be raised print on the note where the bank's name is written and therefore the note shouldn't be entirely smooth when you run a finger across it.

The words should be printed neatly with no blurring.

Most fake coins are easy to spot as either the ribbed edge, colour or image on the coin will look different from normal. The ribbed edge may have the wrong markings, the colour may be too pale or the image of the Queen may look a little blurry or just be the wrong image entirely. So keep your eyes peeled and if the Queen looks a little different on your coin, then it's probably a fake!

In fact, many silver coin fakes are made up of metal alloys rather than silver. If you were to weigh them, you would discover the coin's weight was incorrect, which also points to a fake. There is also a special 'ring' test that you can try . . . balance a silver coin on the tip of your finger and tap it with another coin. All real coins sound the same, but fakes will produce a different 'ring' sound! If you do spot any fakes then officially they are meant to be handed back to the Royal Mint, where the coins are made in the first place.

SPY MONEY FACTS:

- There are currently around **30 million** fake £1 coins in circulation. That's right . . . check your pockets immediately!

- Ever wondered why a vending machine frequently rejects your coins? They are actually very good at identifying fake coins and therefore reject them, which leaves you or your mum and dad desperately trying to find another coin to pay for the parking!

- Although the number of fake bank notes in circulation is actually falling, due to more sophisticated printing methods their quality has improved, making them harder to detect. All you spies are going to have to work even harder!

If you find a fake coin or note in your mum or dad's handbag or wallet, please don't call the police and accuse them of being a mischievous international criminal. They have most probably been handed it by someone else!

THE GREAT SPY WORDSEARCH

By now you've already cracked codes left, right and centre, so how hard can a word search be? Well, naturally, we've made it as hard as possible! See how quickly you can find these spy-related words hidden upwards, downwards, forwards, backwards or diagonally (for extra difficulty) in the grid and award yourself one further **Spy Star** for every word you find . . . remember, you're against the clock as always . . . three, two, one . . . and . . . **GO!**

INTERNATIONAL	GADGET
MORSE	ACADEMY
HANDCUFFS	INVISIBLE
TRANSLATED	KIDNAP
OUTSMART	CAROUSEL

H	E	W	G	T	V	D	C	U	S
M	P	Y	M	E	D	A	C	A	L
W	S	R	F	I	R	O	H	E	G
I	X	L	J	O	B	U	Y	S	B
E	C	D	U	E	C	Z	F	M	J
V	T	S	T	G	S	F	P	K	T
P	E	K	E	W	U	R	T	X	R
L	J	H	G	C	L	P	O	S	A
S	O	F	D	W	A	F	N	M	N
M	Y	N	A	B	N	L	C	O	S
J	A	R	G	M	O	M	E	H	L
H	U	I	D	T	I	G	D	I	A
Q	U	T	V	P	T	J	S	P	T
C	G	N	H	Y	A	B	U	T	E
E	Z	K	L	T	N	N	P	W	D
K	S	X	W	R	R	I	D	E	M
B	F	S	S	L	E	C	B	I	M
T	R	A	M	S	T	U	O	Z	K
O	J	H	D	C	N	Q	L	H	J
K	R	T	H	N	I	V	E	R	O
P	I	N	V	I	S	I	B	L	E

Oh, your mum asked me to pass you this briefcase.
What a lovely lady she is. It's odd, I've never noticed her
deep Russian accent and curly black moustache before.
Anyway, here it is and let's get on with the next section!

RALPH'S GLOSSARY OF HARD WORDS FROM THE BOOK

Just in case you found a few of the words in the book hard to understand, I thought I'd ask aspiring spy Notta Chance to see if she knew their meanings. I'm not entirely sure she's going to make it at this spy game though, so I ALSO asked top international spy Brainia Van Most what these words meant. See if you can tell whose answer is whose! Award yourself a **Spy Star** for every answer you guess correctly. (Although with some of these answers – if you get ANY wrong I think your spying career might be in serious jeopardy!)

Notta Chance

condone

A: Oh, I can't quite remember, but I can tell you how to say it in Morse code of course . . . it should only take a few days for me to work it out!

B: To give approval to, or pardon, or forgive.

curtly

A: Who's Curt? Is he the one on Ralph's chess team?

B: Briefly, shortly, or abruptly.

disgruntled

A: Hmmm . . . well, it has the word 'grunt' in the middle, so it clearly has something to do with pigs or teenage boys?

B: Displeased, grumpy or dissatisfied.

mused

A: I think you mean 'amused' but you've spelled it wrong. Honestly! Thank goodness I'm a spy who ALWAYS checks the detail!

B: To think or comment on thoughtfully.

Brainia Van Most

narcoleptic

A: Errr . . . I could tell you, OF COURSE, but that's my phone. I've got to go on a mission, what a shame!

B: A person who falls suddenly and uncontrollably into a deep sleep. (Not good for spies!)

suave

A: A brand of aftershave? Give us a clue . . . Or a fruit smoothie maybe?

B: Sophisticated or smoothly agreeable.

surmised

A: Ah, yes, now . . . this is spy talk . . . for . . . erm . . . oh, dear, look at the time! I've got to go and, er, rescue someone!

B: Worked out or guessed without strong evidence.

tranquillising

A: Is it a type of dance move? Yes, that sounds about right . . . I'm off tranquillising with my friends!

B: Making something still, peaceful or quiet . . . or, for spies, often involves putting someone to sleep!

By the way, I LOVE your wig! That's the funniest one I've ever seen, but it's a great way to disguise yourself, isn't it? . . . Er, Pardon? . . . That's your REAL hair? Oh, I'm sorry, it's . . . well, lovely! Let's move on to a bit of translating to lighten the mood!

FRENCH GLOSSARY

We didn't bother wasting our time asking Notta Chance about these words from the book, but went straight to international multi-linguist Handy On'oliday for a translation. Some of these are genuine French phrases, but a few have been written in 'franglais' (a mixture of French and 'Anglais' or English) so see if you can use your spy skills to work out which is which!

a) Mais, bien sûr – French for 'but of course'.

b) J'agree – French for 'I agree'.

c) Mes amis – French for 'my friends'.

d) Oui – French for 'yes'.

e) Je suis hungry – French for 'I am hungry'.

f) Très jolie – French for 'very pretty'.

(That's right! Phrases 'b' and 'e' are both written in franglais! The correct way to say 'I agree' in French is 'd'accord' and the correct way to say 'I am hungry' in French is 'J'ai faim'.)

Know any more words in French? Why not use a French dictionary (this will translate English words into French words for you, so also works like code) to help you work out the following phrases in French. Award yourself one **Spy Star** for each sentence you correctly translate (answers appear upside down.)

1. Hello, I'm a spy.	5. Avez-vous le porte-documents?
2. Where is the train station?	4. Quelle heure est-il?
3. Do you like my hat?	3. Aimez-vous mon chapeau?
4. What is the time?	2. Où est la gare?
5. Do you have the briefcase?	1. Bonjour, je suis un espion.

Now before you go, there's someone claiming to be your 'twin brother' at the front door. How nice . . . I didn't realise you had a twin. I'm guessing he was born first though – what with him being six foot four, about eighteen stone and having predominantly grey hair! He must be the elder twin by about what . . . fifty years? Let's move on to the final section and say no more about it!